TIME HOP SWEETS SHOP
Gingerbread with
Abigail Adams

By Reese Everett

Illustrated by Sally Garland

Rourke
Educational Media
rourkeeducationalmedia.com

© 2016 Rourke Educational Media

All rights reserved. No part of this book may be reproduced or utilized in any form or by any means, electronic or mechanical including photocopying, recording, or by any information storage and retrieval system without permission in writing from the publisher.

www.rourkeeducationalmedia.com

Edited by: Keli Sipperley
Cover and Interior layout by: Tara Raymo
Cover and Interior Illustrations by: Sally Garland

Library of Congress PCN Data

Gingerbread with Abigail Adams / Reese Everett
(Time Hop Sweets Shop)
ISBN (hard cover)(alk. paper) 978-1-68191-378-0
ISBN (soft cover) 978-1-68191-420-6
ISBN (e-Book) 978-1-68191-461-9
Library of Congress Control Number: 2015951491

Printed in the United States of America,
North Mankato, Minnesota

Dear Parents and Teachers,

Fiona and Finley are just like any modern-day kids. They help out with the family business, face struggles and triumphs at school, travel through time with important historical figures ...

Well, maybe that part's not so ordinary. At the Time Hop Sweets Shop, anything can happen, at any point in time. The family bakery draws customers from all over the map–and all over the history books. And when Tick Tock the parrot squawks, Fiona and Finley know an adventure is about to begin!

These beginner chapter books are designed to introduce students to important people in U.S. history, turning their accomplishments into adventures that Fiona, Finley, and young readers get to experience right along with them.

Perfect as read-alouds, read-alongs, or independent readers, books in the Time Hop Sweets Shop series were written to delight, inform, and engage your child or students by making each historical figure memorable and relatable. Each book includes a biography, comprehension questions, websites for further reading, and more.

We look forward to our time travels together!

Happy Reading,
Rourke Educational Media

Table of Contents

Chapter 1
Fiona vs. Finley

"I love the smell of victory in the morning!" Finley said, tossing a ball of cookie dough in the air.

Fiona reached over and caught the dough. "The victory you smell is mine," she said.

"No way! I can't even believe you're running for school president. You're too young—and you're a girl," Finley said.

"FINLEY!" Fiona said, hurt.

"Squawk! That was mean! That was mean!" Tick Tock, their parrot, screeched.

Finley blushed. "Sorry," he mumbled. "Didn't mean it."

He sort of meant it. The school election was coming up, and both Fiona and Finley were in the running. It was Finley's last

shot at winning the Old Town Elementary presidency. He'd lost the year before. He was not about to lose this year to his little sister. Not without a fight, anyway.

The family's Sweets Shop was full of customers. Fiona and Finley were supposed to be decorating gingerbread cookies, but mostly they were driving each other crazy.

"When I'm president, I'm going to make a school law that says we must have pizza and ice cream every day," Fiona said.

"When I'm president, I'm going to propose that we have recess every day for at least ..." Finley thought for a moment. "At least three hours!"

"I'm going to have a huge desk at the front of the classroom," Fiona said. "A very president-ish desk. And I will sign important things there. Like my autograph!"

Mom poked her head in the kitchen. "How are those gingerbread cookies coming along?"

"Errrr, almost ready!" Finley fibbed. He blushed again.

"Good! Bring them out front when you're done," she said, disappearing back into the bakery bustle.

Fiona stood on a chair. "Ladies and gentlemen of Old Town," she said. "My opponent tells lies to his own mother!"

"Shhh, get down and help me, Fiona. Hurry!"

"Okay, okay!" Fiona laughed. "Who are these for, anyway?"

"I don't know," Finley said. "Some fancy party."

"When I'm president, I will have many fancy parties, and invite the whole town, and we will have bounce houses, and ponies, and glitter, and—"

"Fiona, who do you think is going to pay for all of that stuff?" Finley interrupted.

"The school government, of course," Fiona said.

Finley shook his head but didn't say anything.

When the gingerbread decorating was finished, they loaded the treats into boxes and carried them out to the shop counter. Dad peeked inside.

"These look great, guys," he said. "What is that one?"

"That's a president gingerbread girl," Fiona said. "That's her presidential top hat, and her presidential cowgirl boots."

Finley sighed and shook his head again. Fiona grinned at him. "Sorry you're gonna lose, big brother!"

"This election is really stirring up the competition between you two, huh?" Dad pulled them both to his side. "Remember, family first, okay?"

Fiona nodded. But all she could think of was winning.

Chapter 2
First, Second, First

"Look at the time! Look at the time!" Tick Tock squawked. This meant a special customer was about to walk in the Sweets Shop's side door. Right on cue, the bells above the door jingled, and a woman walked in.

Fiona thought she looked like royalty. Her bonnet reminded Finley of Easter parties. But it was early November, so that couldn't be right.

"It smells delicious in here," the woman said. "I hope that's my gingerbread I smell!"

"It is!" Finley said.

"Are you a queen from olden times?" Fiona asked.

The woman laughed. "I'm not a queen. But I am the First Lady of the United States. At least in my own time, I am," she said. "I'm Abigail Adams."

"You are? I am going to be president of my school soon!" Fiona said. She felt excited and a little shy at the same time.

"No, I am." Finley crossed his arms and glared at his sister. Then he remembered something. "Abigail Adams? You were the first-ever second lady of the United States, and the second First Lady!"

"That's correct! And the first to live in the president's house in the wild wilderness of Washington, D.C." Abigail said.

Fiona giggled. The Washington, D.C., she'd seen was full of streets and buildings, not wilderness.

"We visited the White House once," Finley said. "It's amazing."

"The White House? Is that what it's called now? I like it," Abigail said. "It's not quite finished in my time. It's a bit cold and damp. But it will be warm this evening! I'm hosting a dinner party. Your gingerbread will be greatly admired."

Mom put the boxes on the counter for Abigail.

"Perhaps, if you wouldn't mind, Fiona and Finley could help me carry them?" Abigail said. "I'd love to have two future presidents attend my party."

"Of course, Lady Adams," Dad said. "Or should I call you Mrs. President?"

Abigail laughed. "People do call me Mrs. President," she said. "But they don't always mean it kindly. Some think I have too much influence on my husband."

"Well, everyone knows behind a great man is an even greater woman!" Dad said, hugging Mom.

"Sheesh, you guys are mushy," Fiona said. "When I'm elected president, I'm going to outlaw mushy stuff."

"Oh, please don't!" Abigail said. "My letters to my husband are often mushy. He is my dearest friend."

"Can we meet him?" Finley said. He agreed with outlawing the mushy stuff, but he kept that to himself. Fiona was his opponent now, and that meant they couldn't agree on anything, right?

"Yes! To November 1800 we go!"

Chapter 3
The Great Castle

Everything whirled around them, like it always did when they time traveled. It didn't matter how many times they'd done it, though. It always made Finley queasy. This time he'd turned down his hearing aids so the roar wouldn't be so loud.

Fiona loved the feeling of cartwheeling through time. But she did not always stick the landing.

"Oomph," she grunted, tripping as her feet hit the ground.

"Don't drop the gingerbread!" Finley said. Fiona stuck her tongue out at him.

Their shorts and T-shirts were traded for old fashioned, formal clothes. Fiona wore a bonnet like Abigail's and a long dress. Finley wore a suit and a top hat. It was itchy, but he thought it made him look important. Fiona hated dresses, but she didn't say anything, because it was a fancy party, after all.

"Welcome to the president's house," Abigail said. "Or, as I like to call it, the great castle!"

The house was huge, but the inside didn't look much like the modern White House. Candlelight and fireplaces illuminated the home because there was no electricity yet. Clothes and sheets hung from lines that crossed one of the rooms.

"This is the East Room," Abigail said. "I'm certain in the future it will serve other purposes, but for now, it is where I hang my laundry."

"Wowza! You do your own laundry?" Fiona asked. She hoped being president meant she wouldn't have chores anymore.

"Yes, I do. I take care of the home, and our children. I also manage our family's finances. I always have," Abigail said. "My husband, John, is away for work so much of the time. I miss him terribly when he's away. We always write letters to each other, though."

Fiona thought about the last time she wrote a letter. She decided it must have been never, because she couldn't remember ever doing it. Then she decided that when she became president, she would write lots of important letters.

"At the Sweets Shop, you said people thought you had too much influence on the president," Finley said. "What did you mean?"

"John always asks for my advice. And I'm always ready to give it to him," Abigail said. "But at this time, women don't have the same rights as men. Men, especially white men, are considered superior. Many think I should not be involved in political discussions at all."

Fiona frowned. She was glad she lived in a time that girls could do anything they wanted. She wondered if Abigail had anything to do with that.

"Tell me more about your plans to become presidents," Abigail said as they set out trays of treats in the dining room for the guests who'd arrive soon.

"We are both running in the election," Finley said. "But only one of us can win. And I'm the oldest, so it has to be me."

"But I've got better plans," Fiona said. "I'm going to make sure there's pizza at lunch every day, and I'm going to get rid of tests, and homework, and—"

Finley snorted. "You are not going to do any of those things. You can't!"

"What are your plans to help the school, if you win the election, Finley?" Abigail asked.

"I'm going to extend recess time, and raise funds so we can go on better field trips, and also maybe raise money for a new bus, because ours smells like moldy cheese. And that's just to start!" Finley said proudly.

"You both have many ideas. But have you considered ways you can use the power of your presidency to help others?"

Fiona and Finley looked at each other. Neither had thought about that. But they knew what Abigail meant.

"I use my position as First Lady to advocate for the rights of women to be educated and own property. I also want to end slavery, a horror our young nation is guilty of engaging in. Everyone has a right to freedom," she said.

"When my husband was drafting the Declaration of Independence, I told him in a letter, John, 'I desire you would remember the ladies and be more generous and favorable to them than your ancestors. Do not put such unlimited power into the hands of the husbands'," Abigail said.

"But women still won't get the right to vote for more than a hundred years," Finley said.

Abigail sighed. "It will take that long? I suppose progress takes time. It also takes people who are dedicated to standing up for and helping others. After all, if we do not lay out ourselves in the service of mankind, whom should we serve?"

A knock at the door meant guests had arrived. Fiona fidgeted nervously. Finley fiddled with his hearing aids.

Abigail left, then returned with a group of men and women.

"Where is the President?" one man asked.

"Right here, kind sir," said a man who entered behind the group. "And who is this?" John asked Abigail, his eyes twinkling. Fiona thought he had a kind face.

"Everyone, this is Fiona and Finley. Both future presidents." Abigail smiled.

A man chuckled. "A woman president? That will never happen," he said. "Women are not fit for leadership."

Finley didn't want to lose the school election, but he also didn't want anyone to think his sister was any less qualified just because she was a girl.

"Fiona is just as fit as you or I," he said.

The men laughed. The women stared. The laughter made Finley's face feel hot.

"My sister is full of great ideas," he said.
"In fact, I am going to vote for her myself!"
Finley swung his arm toward Fiona to hug
her, but something went horribly wrong.

"Yikes, boy, you're on fire!" Finley's sleeve
had caught the flame from a nearby candle,
which fell to the floor, lighting the rug, as
well.

Fiona grabbed a pitcher of water and lunged toward her brother, dousing the flames on his suit. Then she poured the rest on the burning rug.

"Quick thinking, Fiona!" Abigail said.

"I'm so sorry," Finley said.

"It was an accident," Abigail said kindly.

"Not even presidents yet and you've both already left your mark on the President's house," John said, winking at them.

When the party was over, Fiona and Finley thanked the President and First Lady. Then they held hands as they tumbled back into the Sweets Shop.

"Thanks for sticking up for me, big brother," Fiona said.

"Thanks for saving my life back there, little sister," Finley said. "We make a good team. Want to be my vice president?"

"Or you could be mine," Fiona said.

"We'll see," Finley said.

About Abigail Adams

Abigail Smith Adams was born on November 11, 1744, in Weymouth, Massachusetts. She married John Adams in 1764, when she was 19, and immediately became his most trusted advisor. Throughout his political career, which included becoming the first vice president and the second president of the United States, Abigail is the person he turned to for advice.

In the early years of their marriage, John Adams ran a busy law practice. He spent a lot of time away from home. This continued when he became an active member of the American Revolution and the Revolutionary War. During this time, the couple exchanged more than a thousand letters. Their correspondence detailed many important moments in early American history, and Abigail is most famous for her lively writing and forward-thinking viewpoints expressed in them.

Abigail did not have a formal education as a child, because she was girl. In that time, girls did not go to school. But she loved books and read as many as she could, including the works of William Shakespeare. She also studied French. She had many opinions about politics and government. In her letters to John, she urged him to "remember the ladies" as he and other leaders began crafting the new American government after the American Revolution.

In 1797, John was elected president of the United States. In 1800, Abigail and John moved into the new President's House, now known as the White House. She was the first First Lady to live there. Just like in the story, Abigail even used one of the rooms to hang the laundry on clotheslines.

Some people at the time did not like Abigail's influence on her husband. They called her "Mrs. President," which was meant to be an insult. Women at the time were not formally educated, they weren't allowed to own property, and they couldn't vote or hold leadership positions.

These objections didn't stop her, though. Abigail continued to stand up for people who lacked power, such as slaves, women, and the U.S. colonies. She wanted women to have equal rights.

Abigail's political influence didn't end when John's presidency ended. And it didn't end when she died on October 28, 1818. The values she instilled in her family and others lived on in American politics. In 1824, her son John Quincy Adams was elected president.

Comprehension Questions

1. What was the White House originally called? What did Abigail call it?

2. Why did Abigail tell her husband to "remember the ladies"?

3. What other groups of people did she want to help?

Websites to Visit

www.ducksters.com/biog

www.libertyskids.com/arch_who_aadams.
htmlraphy/women_leaders/abigail_adams.php

www.pbs.org/wgbh/amex/adams/
peopleevents/p_adamskids.html

Q & A with Reese Everett

What do you admire most about Abigail Adams?
I admire Abigail for several things. She worked hard to educate herself in a time when girls were not encouraged to be educated. She also stood up for people who did not have any power or influence, which is critical for anyone to do, in my opinion. We should always work to make life better for everyone we can, and everyone should have equal rights under the law, whatever their color and whatever their gender.

What did you find most interesting while researching this book?
It's always interesting to dive into history, and marvel at how much has changed. Women, for example, have only had the right to vote in the United States for less than a hundred years. And now we have so many women in leadership roles that are doing great things for people and the nation. Those changes come about because people like Abigail Adams are willing to stand up for what's right.

If you could time travel like Fiona and Finley, what time period would you like to explore?
I think I would enjoy a trip to Ancient Egypt. I've always been fascinated by Egyptian mythology and ancient cultures, in general.

About the Author

Reese Everett is a writer, mother of four, and supporter of equal rights. She enjoys writing for young people because it gives her the opportunity to learn something new every day. When she's not writing, she's usually watching her kids play sports, or trying to talk them into some adventure. The beach is her favorite place in the world.

About the Illustrator

Sally Anne Garland was born in Hereford England and moved to the Highlands of Scotland at the age of three. She studied Illustration at Edinburgh College of Art before moving to Glasgow where she now lives with her partner and young son.